## Dragon Slayers' Academy 1

# THE NEW KID
# AT SCHOOL

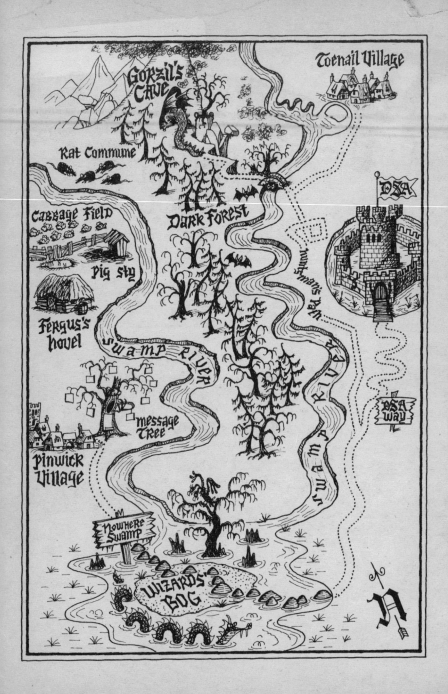

# Dragon Slayers' Academy 1

# THE NEW KID
# AT SCHOOL

## By K.H. McMullan
## Illustrated by Bill Basso

GROSSET & DUNLAP • NEW YORK

For Mrs. Roché-Albert
and all the great kids
in her class at P.S. 116
—K.H. McM.

*Library of Congress Cataloging-in-Publication Data*
McMullan, K.H.
   The new kid at school / by K.H. McMullan ; illustrated by Bill Basso.
      p.  cm. — (Dragon Slayers' Academy ; 1)
   Summary: Wiglaf is off to Dragon Slayers' Academy and in for a first day of school he will never forget.
   [1. Dragons—Fiction.  2. First day of school—Fiction.  3. Schools—Fiction.]
I. Basso, Bill, ill.  II. Title.  III. Series: McMullan, K.H. Dragon Slayers' Academy; 1.
PZ7.M47879Ne  1997                                                                                    97-15520
[E] — dc21                                                                                                   CIP
                                                                                                              AC
ISBN 0-448-41592-5 (pbk) A B C E F G H I J
ISBN 0-448-41727-8 (GB) A B C E F G H I J

Reprinted by arrangement with Grosset & Dunlap, Inc.,
a member of The Putnam & Grosset Group.
10  9  8  7  6  5  4  3  2  1

# Chapter I

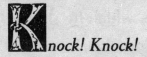nock! Knock!

"Who's there?" Fergus bellowed from inside the hovel.

"A poor minstrel!" came a voice from out in the blizzard.

"A poor minstrel who?" Fergus called.

"Please! I am freezing!" cried the minstrel. "This is no time for a joke!"

"Pity!" Fergus yelled. "There's nothing I like better than a good knock-knock!"

He yanked open the door. There stood a snow-covered man with a lute and a pack slung over his shoulder. Icicles hung from his nose and ears. His lips were blue from the cold.

"Be gone, varlet!" Fergus shouted through his dirty yellow beard. "There is no room here!"

Fergus spoke the truth. His whole hovel was but one cramped room, which he shared with his wife, Molwena, and their thirteen sons.

Twelve of these sons were big, beefy lads with greasy yellow hair like their father's. They scowled out the door at the minstrel, shouting, "Be gone! Be gone!"

But the third-eldest son, Wiglaf, was different from his brothers. He was small for his age. He had hair the color of carrots. And he could not bear to see any creature suffer.

When Fergus reached out to slam the door in the shivering minstrel's face, Wiglaf grabbed his arm.

"Wait, Father!" he said. "Could not the minstrel sleep in the pigsty?"

"I sing songs and tell fortunes," the minstrel offered.

"Songs? Fortunes?" Fergus growled. "Pig droppings!"

"I also chop wood, shovel snow, slop pigs, rake dung, scrub floors, and wash dishes," the minstrel added quickly.

"Oh, but we have Wiglaf to do all that," Molwena told him.

"Please!" the minstrel begged through his chattering teeth. "There must be *something* I can do in return for a roof over my head."

Fergus scratched his beard and tried to think.

"He might kill rats for us, Fergus," Molwena suggested. "Wiglaf won't do that."

"Wiglaf feels sorry for the rats," one of the younger brothers told the minstrel.

"Wiglaf won't squish a cockroach," another

brother tattled. "He won't even swat a fly."

"Wiggie never wants to kill anything," complained a third. "I was pulling the legs off a spider once, and—"

"I have it!" Fergus bellowed suddenly. "The minstrel can kill rats to earn his keep!" He grinned. "Show him to the sty, Wiglaf!"

So Wiglaf did just that. And later on he took a bowl of Molwena's cabbage soup out to the minstrel for his supper.

"Ah! Hot soup to warm my cold bones!" The minstrel took a sip. "Gaaach!" he cried, and spat it out.

"It is foul-tasting at first," Wiglaf admitted. "But you'll get used to it."

"I must or I shall starve," the minstrel said. "Talk to me, lad, while I try to get it down." Then he held his nose and jammed a spoonful into his mouth.

"You are lucky to bed out here with the pigs," Wiglaf told him. "The sty smells far better than our hovel, for my father believes that bathing causes madness. And Daisy, here"—he patted the head of a plump young pig sitting next to him—"she is my best friend. And far better company than my brothers. They only like to fight and bloody each other's noses."

Wiglaf rubbed his own nose. It was still tender from one of his brother's fists.

"They gang up on me something awful," he added. "Then they call me a blister and a runt because I will not fight back. I know it is foolish," he went on, "but sometimes I dream that one day I will become a mighty hero. Would not *that* surprise my brothers!"

"No doubt it would," the minstrel said. He jammed one last spoonful of soup into his mouth. Then he burped. "Ah! That's better. Now, my boy, I know some tales of mighty heroes. Would you care to hear one?"

"I would, indeed!" Wiglaf exclaimed.

No one had ever told Wiglaf a tale before. Oh, Molwena sometimes told him what she would do to him if he did not wash the dishes. And Fergus often told him how he was no use at all in the cabbage fields. But those tales were not so much fun to hear.

Wiglaf settled down in the straw next to his pig to listen. The tale was indeed about a mighty hero. A hero who tried to slay a dragon named Gorzil.

When at last the minstrel came to the end, his voice dropped low. "Then Gorzil roared a roar of thunder. Bolts of lightning shot from his nose. And from out of the fire and smoke came a CRUNCH...CRUNCH...CRUNCH! And a mighty GULP!

"When the smoke cleared, the knight and his steed were gone," the minstrel said. "But Gorzil was sitting high on his pile of gold— using the knight's own sword for a toothpick."

"No!" cried Wiglaf.

"'Tis true," the minstrel told the boy. "My grandfather was a dragon hunter. He saw it happen with his own two eyes—well, with his one good eye, anyway."

"Pray, tell," Wiglaf asked, "who finally killed this dragon?"

"Oh, Gorzil is still very much alive." The minstrel grew thoughtful. "My grandfather told me that every dragon has a secret weakness. Take Old Snart, for instance. For years, that dragon set fire to villages for sport. Then one day Sir Gilford stuck out his tongue and said, 'Nonny-nonny poo-poo, you old sissy!' Well, Old Snart hated to be teased. He began whimpering and crying until he collapsed in a pool of tears. He hardly noticed when Sir Gilford sliced off his head."

"And what is the dragon Gorzil's weakness?" Wiglaf asked.

"That," said the minstrel, "no one knows."
He picked up his lute. "I have written a song
about Gorzil. Listen:

"*Gorzil is a dragon, a greedy one is he,*
   *From his jaws of terror, villagers do flee.*
   *Gorzil burps up clouds of smoke,*
   *Shoots lightning from his snout....*
   *Where, oh, where's the hero*
   *Who'll find his secret out?*"

From that night on, Wiglaf brought the
minstrel a bowl of cabbage soup for supper.
In return, the minstrel told Wiglaf many a
dragon tale. And he taught the boy many a
useful skill: how to stand on his head; how to
wiggle his ears; and how to imitate the call of
a lovesick toad.

By the time the snow began to melt, he had
even taught the boy how to read and write.

Then one spring morning, Wiglaf brought the pigs their slop and found the minstrel packing.

"Are you off for good?" Wiglaf asked sadly.

"Aye, lad. A minstrel must wander," the minstrel explained. "And"—he burped—"eat something besides cabbage soup. But here, give me your hand. Before I go, I shall tell your fortune."

Wiglaf held out his palm. The minstrel studied it for a long time.

"What do you see?" Wiglaf finally asked.

"Something I never thought to see," the minstrel replied. "The lines on your palm say that you were born to be a mighty hero!"

"Me?" Wiglaf cried. "Are you sure?"

The minstrel nodded. "In all my years of telling fortunes, I have never been wrong."

"Imagine!" Wiglaf exclaimed. "But what brave deed will I do?"

"That," said the minstrel, "you must discover for yourself. Now I must be off. I shall miss you, Wiglaf."

"Wait!" Wiglaf said. He reached into his tunic and pulled out a tattered piece of cloth. "This is all I have left of...well, of something I had when I was very young. I carry it with me always, for good luck." He held the rag out to the minstrel. "Here. I should like you to have it."

"Keep your good-luck charm, Wiglaf," the minstrel said, shouldering his lute. "The road a hero travels is never an easy one. I fear you shall need much luck."

And with that he was gone.

# Chapter 2

"**K**nock! Knock!" Fergus bellowed one fine summer morning at the breakfast table.

Wiglaf didn't answer. He poked at his cabbage pancake, lost in his own thoughts.

It had been months since the minstrel went away. And as far as Wiglaf could tell, he had not become a hero. True, he had saved a chipmunk from drowning in the pigs' water trough. And he had rescued six spiders from his brothers' cruel hands. But surely these were not the deeds of a mighty hero.

Wiglaf kept brooding. He never noticed Fergus bending down close to his ear.

"KNOCK! KNOCK!" Fergus shouted.

Wiglaf jumped. "Who—who's there?"

"Harry!" Fergus cried.

"Harry who?" asked Wiglaf.

"Harry up and eat your pancakes!" Fergus roared. "We go to the Pinwick Fair today!"

"Hooray!" yelled one of Wiglaf's little brothers. "Jugglers and lepers! Let us be off!"

"And so we shall be," Molwena promised, "as soon as Wiglaf does the dishes."

"We could be off sooner if someone dried," Wiglaf hinted.

"Nah," said the eldest brother. "We'll wait."

And so Wiglaf scrubbed the dishes. Then he dried them. Then he put them away.

At last the family set off for the village.

Just outside Pinwick, Fergus stopped beside the village message tree. He squinted at a new notice tacked to its trunk.

"Wiglaf!" Fergus shouted. "The minstrel showed you how to make sense of these squiggles. Tell us what this sign says!"

Wiglaf stepped up and read: "Dragon Slayers' Academy."

Fergus frowned. "Acada...*what?*"

"Academy," Wiglaf repeated. "It means school."

"I know *that*," his father said. "Go on."

"We teach our students to slay dragons," Wiglaf read.

*Slay dragons?* Wiglaf thought with growing interest. *Heroes slayed dragons!*

"And," he read on, "they bring the dragons' hoards home to *you!*"

"The dragons' hoards?" Fergus scratched his armpit thoughtfully. "That would be... what?"

"Gold and jewels, most likely," Wiglaf replied.

"Blazing King Ken's britches!" Fergus roared. "Read it all!" Which is just what Wiglaf was dying to do:

Is there a lazy lad hanging about your hovel? Is he eating more than his share of your good cabbage soup? Don't you wish he could earn his keep?

"I'll say," snorted Molwena.

Dragon Slayers' Academy is your answer! Feast your eyes on just a few of our classes:

- How to Stalk a Fire-Breather
- How to Get Close to a Dragon
- How to Get Even Closer
- How to Get Really, Really Close
- 101 Ways to Slay

Best of all, we will teach your boy how to bring a dragon's golden hoard home to you!

Just look at what some of our fine lads have done:

### Baldrick the Bold
Baldrick slew three dragons! With their golden hoards, he bought his lucky parents a 450-room castle!

"That would do for us," Molwena muttered.

### Torblad the Terrible
Two kills. Two hoards. Now his mum and pop just lie about and watch other folk work.

"Oh, boy!" said Fergus.

### Angus the Avenger
Angus slew a whole nest of dragon young! His parents now dress in nothing but silk and velvet.

"Do they, now?!" Molwena exclaimed. "I wonder how much this school costs."

*The fee? Only 7 pennies! (Plus a teensy part of each hoard.) Send us your sons! We turn useless lads into HEROES who go for the gold!*

*Signed,*
*Mordred the Marvelous, Headmaster, DSA (Located just off Huntsman's Path, east of the Dark Forest)*

*Dragon slaying,* thought Wiglaf. It sounded pretty gruesome. But dragons were evil. They deserved to be slain—didn't they? And who slew them? Mighty heroes, that's who!

Maps tacked to the tree showed the way from Pinwick to Dragon Slayers' Academy. Wiglaf pulled one off and stared at it. Here was a path he might follow to become a hero!

"Father?" Wiglaf began eagerly, "I would—"

"Quiet!" Fergus barked. He turned to his eldest son. "Do you want to go to the acad... to the school?" he asked him.

The eldest picked at a scab on his ear. "Would I get in trouble for fighting and knocking other boys' teeth out?" he asked.

Fergus nodded. "You might."

"I wouldn't like that," the eldest declared.

Wiglaf tried again. "Father, I—"

"Shush!" Fergus turned to his second-eldest. "Do you want to go to the school?" he asked him.

The second-eldest scratched a bedbug bite on his neck. "Would I have to comb my hair and change my britches?" he asked.

Fergus nodded again. "Most likely."

"Then I won't go," the second-eldest said.

"I will, Father!" Wiglaf exclaimed. "Pray, send me!"

But Fergus only rolled his eyes and turned to his fourth-eldest. "You're a big, strapping lad," he began. "How would you—"

"Wait, Father!" Wiglaf cut in. "Think on this: If I slay a dragon, I shall bring you a mountain of gold! You would like that, would you not?"

"Yes...." Fergus nodded slowly.

"And if the dragon gets the better of me?" Wiglaf went on. "Well, you say I am no use to you in the cabbage fields anyway."

"Hmm...." Fergus tugged at a chicken bone that had been tangled in his beard all week. "I have it!" he roared at last. "I shall send *Wiglaf* to the dragon school! He is no use to me in the cabbage fields anyway!"

"That's a fine idea, Fergus," Molwena put in. "But what about the seven pennies? Where would we get that kind of money?"

Fergus shrugged. "That pig of his should bring seven pennies."

"You mean, sell Daisy?" Wiglaf cried.

Wiglaf's younger brother wiped his nose on

his sleeve. "Daddy?" he said. "When Wiglaf goes, can I have his goatskin to sleep under?"

"Yes, all right," replied their father.

"But—" Wiglaf began.

"Can I have his spoon, then?" asked his even younger brother.

"Yes, yes," answered Fergus.

"Can I have his boots?" asked his still younger brother. "And his britches and his tunic?"

"Wait!" Wiglaf cried. "I'm not dead, am I? I still need my clothes! And I shall never sell Daisy! Never!"

"Oh, do be quiet," Molwena scolded. "How else are you going to get seven pennies?"

Wiglaf folded his arms across his chest. "I shall find a way."

"Mommy," one of the younger brothers whined, "I want to go to the fair! I want to see the two-headed calf."

"Of course you do!" Molwena exclaimed.

"And we don't want to miss the hanging." She turned away from the tree, and the rest of the family followed.

All but Wiglaf. He straggled behind, thinking. He was going away to Dragon Slayers' Academy! And, somehow, he was going to keep Daisy by his side.

Wiglaf smiled. At last he was on his way to becoming a mighty hero.

# Chapter 3

"Well, farewell!" Wiglaf said the next morning at dawn. Fergus and Molwena and a few of his brothers had gotten up to see him off.

Fergus slapped Wiglaf on the back and roared, "Knock! Knock!"

"Who's there?" called a little brother.

"Oliver!" said Fergus.

"Oliver who?" asked another little brother.

"Oliver troubles will be over when Wiglaf comes home with the gold!" Fergus cried. He slapped him on the back again.

"Off you go," Molwena said. "Get a good price for the pig."

"And don't come home without the gold!" Fergus added.

Wiglaf picked up his pack. Inside were six cabbage dumplings, a loaf of cabbage bread, and a pickled cabbage tart. He had also put in a length of rope, the map, and his lucky rag.

"Ready, Daisy?" Wiglaf asked.

The faithful pig glanced up at him and wagged her curly tail. Then the two of them set off for Dragon Slayers' Academy.

They walked south all morning. Around noon, they came to Nowhere Swamp. The minstrel had told Wiglaf tales of this spot. Hungry serpents lurked in the slimy water. Hungry vultures circled overhead. Mad hermits lived in every cave and hollow tree. And most of them were hungry, too.

But worst of all was the quicksand. It was so quick it could suck a boy down—*slurp!*—before he could cry for help. A traveler had to be very careful to get across it with his life.

Wiglaf studied his map closely. "We must cross here, Daisy," he said. "I shall carry you."

Wiglaf picked up the pig and started along the spine of rocks jutting out from the quicksand. Wiglaf knew that one false step and—*slurp!*—he would never be a hero.

On a big, flat rock halfway across, Wiglaf stopped. He put Daisy down and searched the swamp to see how far they still had to go.

"Daisy!" Wiglaf cried. "A pointed hat is sinking in the quicksand! And look! There is a *head* beneath the hat!"

Daisy squealed in alarm.

Wiglaf cupped his hands to his mouth. "Stay where you are!" he shouted to the head. "I shall save you!"

Wiglaf grabbed the rope from his pack. His heart thumped. He never thought that he would be a hero *this* soon! But before he could throw the rope, the hat and head started to rise.

Wiglaf watched, amazed, as a man with a long white beard floated up, out of the sand. He wore a wide-sleeved blue robe dotted with silver stars. He glided over the quicksand toward Wiglaf and Daisy.

Now Daisy squealed in fright.

The man came to a stop in front of Wiglaf. "Don't you have anything better to do than annoy me?" he grumbled. "And turn off that pig!"

Instantly, Daisy stopped squealing.

"I am sorry," Wiglaf managed. "Are—are you a wizard?"

"No, I'm a fairy princess!" the man snapped. "Of course I'm a wizard. You know anyone else who wears a long blue robe with stars on it? I don't think so. Zelnoc's the name," he went on. "And your name is...wait." The wizard squeezed his eyes shut. "Don't tell me. It's coming. Ah! I have it. Wigwam! No...Waglump!"

"Close," Wiglaf said. "I am Wiglaf. And this is my pig, Daisy."

"Charmed." The wizard gave a little wave. "Now, Wuglop, what was all that yelling about? And what's with the rope?"

"I was going to rescue you from the quicksand," Wiglaf explained.

Zelnoc shook his head. "Do you know nothing of wizards, my boy? I wasn't sinking. I was in for repairs. This part of the swamp is known as Wizards' Bog. The quicksand here has strong powers. You see, sometimes my spells go wrong...." He shrugged. "It's not your problem. So tell me. What are you doing out here in the middle of Nowhere?"

"I am on my way to Dragon Slayers' Academy," Wiglaf said proudly.

"You're kidding!" Zelnoc exclaimed. "*You* are a dragon slayer?"

"Not yet," Wiglaf admitted. "But a minstrel told my fortune. He said that I was born to be a hero. And heroes slay dragons, do they not?"

"Some do, I suppose," the wizard said. "Well, I wish you luck, Wicklamp. And speaking of wishes, what'll it be?"

"I beg your pardon?" Wiglaf said.

"Your wish!" Zelnoc repeated. "You *did* interrupt me, it's true. But you meant well. And Wizard Rule Number 364 says every good deed must be rewarded. So wish away, Wigloop. But make it snappy. I haven't got all day."

"All right," Wiglaf agreed. "I wish for... seven pennies!"

Zelnoc shook his head. "Sorry, kid. Wizards never carry cash."

"I see." Wiglaf thought for a moment. Then he said, "How about a suit of armor?"

"No, no, no," the wizard scolded. "Only *knights* wear armor!"

Wiglaf sighed. "What should I wish for?"

"A sword," Zelnoc told him.

"All right," said Wiglaf. "I wish for a sword."

"An excellent choice!" exclaimed the wizard. "And have I got a sword for you!"

Zelnoc reached up his left sleeve and pulled out a stumpy metal blade. It was badly bent, dented, and covered with rust.

"This is Surekill," Zelnoc said. "It was made for dragon slaying. It has great power."

"Oh, is it a magic sword?" Wiglaf asked hopefully.

"Would I give you any other kind?" Zelnoc rolled his eyes. "Now, here's what you do. Point Surekill at your enemy and say..." The wizard frowned. "What is it, now? 'Surekill, go get 'em!'? No... 'Surekill, do your thing!'? No. But it's something like that. Anyway, when you do get it right, Surekill will leap from your hand and obey."

"Uh...thank you," Wiglaf said, taking the weapon and tucking it into his belt. He supposed a rusty, dented sword was better than no sword at all.

Zelnoc glanced at Daisy. "What about the pig?" he asked. "Does she have a wish?"

"If only she could talk, she might tell you," Wiglaf answered.

"Talk?" Zelnoc's eyes lit up. "I have just the thing! My speech spell!"

The wizard pushed up his sleeves, stretched his hands toward Daisy, and began to chant: "Oink-a-la, doink-a-la, fee fi fig! This pig shall be a talking pig!"

Daisy blinked, and very softly she said, "Iglaf-Way?"

"She speaks!" Wiglaf cried. "Yet in what strange tongue?"

"Maybe Greek?" the wizard guessed.

"E-may, alking-tay!" Daisy burbled happily.

"I know!" Wiglaf exclaimed. "'Tis Pig Latin!"

"Excuse me?" Zelnoc said.

"Pig Latin," Wiglaf said. "You know—where you take the first sound in a word and put it at the end. Then you add the 'ay' sound. Pig becomes 'ig-pay.' Do you see?"

"Pig Latin, my foot!" Zelnoc moaned. "My spell went wrong!"

"O-nay idding-kay!" Daisy scoffed.

"Stop, pig!" Zelnoc cried. "That crazy language makes my beard twitch." He shuddered. "I'm in worse shape than I thought. And the Wizards' Convention is only two weeks away."

Zelnoc turned and began gliding back to the center of the bog.

"Good-bye, Waglap!" he called. "Good luck with the dragons!"

"Good-bye!" Wiglaf called back.

"O-say ong-lay!" Daisy squealed.

Then, with a loud *slurp*, the quicksand swallowed up the wizard, this time hat and all.

# Chapter 4

Wiglaf checked his map by the light of the full moon. Yes, this had to be the place—Dragon Slayers' Academy.

"In truth, this is not what I expected," Wiglaf muttered.

"Uck-yay," Daisy agreed.

Wiglaf and Daisy stood at the edge of a moat filled with greenish, foul-smelling water. It reminded Wiglaf, in many ways, of Molwena's cabbage soup.

A rickety drawbridge led over the water to a gatehouse set in the middle of the broken-down castle wall. A tattered blue banner waved above the door. Bold letters on it spelled out DSA.

Wiglaf drew a deep breath and started across the drawbridge. Daisy trotted at his side.

Wiglaf pulled a chain by the gatehouse door. A bell sounded from deep within.

After a time, the door cracked open. A short man with big eyes stared out at the travelers. He held a torch in one hand.

"Yes?" he said.

"I am Wiglaf, sir," Wiglaf offered. "I am here to study."

"Welcome to DSA!" the man said, opening the door. Wiglaf saw that he wore an apron. "Odd time to arrive, midnight," the man went on. "And school started two weeks ago. But no matter. First things first." He held out his hand. "Seven pennies, please."

"Alas," Wiglaf sighed. "I have no pennies."

The door began to close.

"Wait, sir!" he called. "I—I have half a cabbage dumpling!"

The door banged shut.

"I am a willing worker!" Wiglaf added. "I wash dishes and—"

The door opened a few inches. The man stuck his head out.

"You are skilled at washing dishes?" he asked.

Wiglaf nodded. "Very skilled."

"Well, that suits me better than seven pennies any day." The man opened wide the door. "Come in, come in. I am Frypot, school cook. And former dishwasher."

"Oh, I thank you, kind sir!" Wiglaf exclaimed.

"But say not a word of this to Headmaster Mordred," Frypot warned. "He will put the thumbscrews to me if he finds out."

"Not a word, sir," Wiglaf promised. Then he and Daisy started through the door.

"Hold up now!" Frypot cried. "No pigs allowed!"

"But, sir," Wiglaf began. "This is no ordinary pig! Just listen. Daisy, say hello to the kind man."

"Ello-hay, Ypot-Fray!" Daisy said.

"Zounds!" Frypot exclaimed. "A pig that speaks Pig Latin!"

Frypot knelt down next to Daisy.

"Ello-hay, iggy-pay," he said slowly and loudly. "Oh, I shall make you a comfy pallet in the henhouse! Yes, just as soon as I sign in our new dishwasher—er, I mean student."

Then Frypot lit the way through the gatehouse, across the castle yard, and up a stone stairway into the crumbling castle.

Just inside the door, Frypot stuck his torch into a holder on the wall. Then he sat down at a desk and opened a thick book.

"Full name?" he asked.

"Wiglaf of Pinwick."

"Age?"

"This shall be my twelfth summer."

"Skills?"

"Washing dishes," began Wiglaf, "slopping pigs, raking dung—"

"I meant any skills that might be useful in dragon slaying," Frypot said.

Wiglaf thought for a moment. "Nothing comes to mind," he answered.

"Class I, then." Frypot shut the book. He opened a cupboard and took out a blue tunic and a helmet. White letters on the tunic spelled out DSA. He gave them to Wiglaf. "Your uniform," he said.

"The kitchen's that way," Frypot added, handing Wiglaf the torch. "You can start on the dishes while I settle your pig."

Then the cook led Daisy toward the door. "Ome-cay, iggy-pay," he said, "and tell me how you came by your enchantment. I never cook bacon, you know. Well, hardly ever...."

"What a poor sword!" Wiglaf heard someone exclaim.

He half-opened one eye. He had not had much sleep. Frypot had not told him how very, *very* many dirty dishes there would be.

Now Wiglaf saw two boys in DSA tunics standing at the foot of his cot. One was sandy-haired and plump. The other had straight brown hair and a serious face. He was holding Surekill.

"Have you ever drawn this sword in battle?" the boy asked.

"No," Wiglaf answered.

"Have you sliced off anyone's head with it?"

"Of course not!" Wiglaf exclaimed.

"And I'll wager you have never killed a dragon with it, either."

"No," Wiglaf admitted. "But the sword is called Surekill," he added. "So perhaps I shall. I am called Wiglaf."

"I am Eric." The boy tossed Surekill back onto Wiglaf's cot. "I sleep there." He pointed to the far side of the room.

Wiglaf turned to see one of many lumpy cots just like his own. On the wall above it hung a certificate which read: SIR LANCELOT FAN CLUB. Next to that hung a tapestry. It showed a knight plunging a sword into a dragon. Blood gushed from the dragon's side. *Yuck!* thought Wiglaf.

"I have not yet killed a dragon," Eric was saying. "But soon I shall. Not for the gold, but to rid the world of evil! I want—"

"Pray, save it, Eric," the plump boy cut in.

"Or we shall miss breakfast." He turned to Wiglaf, adding, "Don't worry. We are not all so eager as Eric."

Wiglaf put on his DSA tunic and helmet, and followed his roommates to a huge dining hall.

Boys of all sizes sat at long wooden tables labeled "Class I," "Class II," and "Class III." A big boy was tossing slices of burnt toast through the air. Other boys punched and poked and pinched each other for the honor of catching them.

The sight made Wiglaf feel a little homesick.

Wiglaf got in line and picked up his tray.

"What's for breakfast?" he asked Eric.

"Fried eel on toast," Eric replied as he took a heaping plateful.

*"Eel?"* Wiglaf cried.

Eric nodded. "Mordred says eating eel is

part of our training," he explained. "Dragon hunters must learn to live on what can be found near a dragon's lair."

The boys carried their trays to the Class I table. Then Wiglaf watched as Eric scooped up a spoonful of greasy eel and eagerly stuffed it into his mouth.

"Ugh!" Wiglaf groaned. "How do dragon hunters do it?"

The plump boy leaned over toward him. "They don't," he whispered. "Eels live in the castle moat, so they do not cost Mordred a cent. *That* is the real reason we are served eel so often."

"How often?" Wiglaf asked in dismay.

"Too often," the boy replied. "By the way, I am Angus."

Wiglaf stared in awe. "Angus the Avenger?"

"Oh, you saw the notice." Angus smiled shyly. "Mordred only made me sound fierce to attract fierce pupils to his school."

"Then...you never killed a nest of dragon young?" Wiglaf asked.

"Not exactly," Angus admitted. "I stumbled over an old dragon nest in the forest once and squashed some rotten eggs. Whew! Did they ever stink!" He waved a hand in front of his nose. "It took weeks to get the slimy goo off my boots."

"Then Torblad the Terrible and Baldrick the Bold...?" Wiglaf began.

Angus shook his head. "I am afraid my Uncle Mordred sometimes stretches the truth."

"The headmaster is your uncle?" Wiglaf exclaimed. "Imagine! So has anybody here ever killed a dragon?"

"Not yet," Eric piped up. "But soon someone shall—and that someone shall be me!"

*Clang! Clang!* A bell sounded and Eric slurped up the tail of his eel.

"Finish up," Angus advised Wiglaf.

"Stalking a Fire-Breather Class begins in five minutes. And it is way over in the East Tower."

Wiglaf stared at his fried eel on toast—now cold and gray. Then he left it on his plate and hurried after Angus and Eric.

# Chapter 5

Wiglaf, Eric, and Angus rushed along the castle hallways until they came to a spiraling stone staircase. They ran up the steps, two at a time. When they reached the top of the East Tower, they were panting for breath.

Several boys stood at a window, pulling on a rope. Angus and Eric joined them.

Wiglaf, too, began to pull. "What are we raising?" he asked. "It is quite heavy."

"'Tis Sir Mort," Angus replied. "Our teacher. He has a hard time walking up stairs."

In a moment, Wiglaf saw why. A helmeted head appeared at the window. The boys reached out to pull their teacher in. And Sir Mort crashed to the classroom floor—wearing a full suit of armor.

The boys helped him to his feet.

"Stalking a fire-breather is no easy matter, lads," the old knight began lecturing as he lurched and clattered to the front of the room. "Dragons can hear you coming from miles away. Especially if you have on armor. Clanks something awful."

"Sir?" Eric called. "What about a dragon's sense of smell?"

"Oh, they smell all right." Sir Mort nodded thoughtfully. "Like old cheese, most of them. But I slew a dragon once that smelled exactly like my red wool socks when I wear 'em too long and the mold sets in."

Eric tried again. "I meant, can a dragon smell a dragon hunter?"

"Ah! Good question!" Sir Mort exclaimed. "That's how you learn, lads! By asking questions!" He looked around the room. "Are there any more questions?"

A tall, scared-looking boy raised his hand. "How close dare we stalk a dragon without danger?" he asked in a shaky voice.

"*That*," Angus whispered to Wiglaf, "is Torblad the Terrible."

"How close!" Sir Mort exclaimed. "An excellent question. Excellent! You will go far, lad! Next question?"

Eric's hand shot up again. *He certainly is eager,* Wiglaf thought.

"Yesterday you said we must stalk different dragons in different ways," Eric said. "Can you give us an example?"

"Certainly I can." Sir Mort nodded, smiling. "Easy as pie."

Eric and the rest of the class waited. But Sir Mort only kept nodding and smiling.

"Sir?" Eric said at last. "Will you *show* us what you mean?"

"Good idea!" The old knight jangled to the center of the room.

"Take cave-dwelling dragons. They have excellent hearing," Sir Mort explained. "So they must be approached on the sly. I use what I call the Slide 'n' Glide. I stand sideways to the cave like this." Sir Mort turned sideways to the class. "And I slide my right foot out, like this." Sir Mort slid his right foot out.

Unfortunately, the old stone floors of the castle were far smoother than the ground outside a dragon's cave. Sir Mort's boot kept sliding and sliding...and sliding. Until the old knight clanked to the floor in a perfect split. His visor slammed down over his face.

"Hoist me up, lads!" Sir Mort cried in a muffled voice.

Eric and two other boys gripped their teacher under the arms and pulled him up.

"Ah, that's better." Sir Mort pushed his

visor back up. "Slippery devils, these boots. Reminds me of the time I stalked the dragon Fiffnir. Have I shown you the wound Fiffnir gave me? Nasty wound it is, too."

Sir Mort bent down. He began struggling to pull off the left boot of his armor.

In the distance a bell rang.

Angus spoke up. "Sir Mort, class is over."

"Devilish tight, this boot," Sir Mort grumbled.

"Sir, we must go to Slaying Class now," Angus continued. "Coach Plungett gets vexed if we are late."

"Go then, lads. Go!" Sir Mort said. "My wound will wait. Got it the year of the grasshopper plague. No, the year before. Couldn't have walked to Constantinople. Not with this wound. No, it must have been..."

Quietly, Wiglaf followed Angus and Eric and the other future dragon slayers down the spiral staircase. He was amazed at how much he had learned of dragon stalking in one short morning!

"Step it up, lads!" Coach Plungett called as Class I ran out into the castle yard. The large man's long brown pageboy-style hair blew gently in the breeze. "Ten laps around the castle," he ordered. "Can't kill a dragon if you're not in shape!"

By lap three, Eric was way ahead of the others. Wiglaf was way behind. He began to worry that slopping pigs and washing dishes had not prepared him well for dragon slaying.

But after the laps, the coach ordered the boys to take a deep breath and hold it for the count of fifty.

"If a dragon spews out poison," he told them, "the longer you can hold your breath, the better. Ready? And! One...two...three...."

Wiglaf smiled as he held his breath. Living

in the smelly hovel with his unwashed family had given him plenty of practice at this skill! He alone made it to the count of fifty.

"Good work!" Coach Plungett told him. "Now before we start slaying, why don't you give the DSA cheer for our new boy? Belt it out now, boys!"

At once, the whole class began shouting at the top of their lungs:

> *"Rooty-toot-ho! Rooty-toot-hey!*
> *We are the boys from DSA!*
> *We slay dragons, yes we do!*
> *Big ones! Bony ones! Fat ones, too!*
> *We slay dragons, young and old!*
> *We slay dragons, grab their gold!*
> *Yea! Yea! For good old DSA—Hey!"*

"Hey!" Coach clapped at the end of the cheer. "All right now, line up in front of Old Blodgett. Quickly, lads. Go on!"

Wiglaf and the others lined up in front of a

large dragon. It wasn't a real dragon, of course. Old Blodgett was only a wooden one covered with cloth and stuffed with straw.

"Slaying is the most important class here at DSA," Coach told the boys. "You can find a dragon. You can stalk a dragon. But if you cannot *slay* a dragon, you cannot get a hoard.

"Today we shall practice Slaying Method Number Seven, the Throat Thrust. Aim here." Coach Plungett pointed the tip of his sword just under Old Blodgett's chin where a target had been painted. "Not many scales in that spot. Watch me now!"

Coach Plungett faced the false dragon. He drew his weapon, galloped a few steps, and with a toss of his brown pageboy, thrust his sword deep into the dragon's neck.

Wiglaf cringed. He knew that no blood would spill from this dragon. Still his stomach did flip-flops.

Wiglaf watched with growing dread as each

boy took a turn stabbing the practice dragon. When his turn came, he drew Surekill, galloped toward the dragon, and stopped.

"Go on, boy!" Coach Plungett urged him.

Wiglaf backed up. He gripped Surekill more tightly. He stared at the target on the dragon's throat. He galloped forward again ...and stopped.

"Blazing King Ken's britches!" Coach cried. "Aim here!" He pointed at the target.

Wiglaf backed up once more. He swallowed. If he could not plunge his sword into this dummy dragon, what hope did he have of ever slaying a *real* one? Wiglaf took a step toward Old Blodgett. Then another. And another.

"I cannot watch!" Coach Plungett moaned. He turned away in disgust.

But Wiglaf kept on. Faster and faster he came. At the last minute, he closed his eyes.

"Haiii-yah!" He thrust Surekill up toward the dragon's chin.

But somehow Wiglaf missed. He went flying past the practice dragon and landed on a bale of straw. His eyes popped open. Around him, boys were hooting and pointing.

Wiglaf glanced at Surekill. His heart nearly stopped. He had missed the practice dragon. But he had speared some small, brown, furry creature! There it was, stuck on the end of his sword!

*Why is everyone laughing,* Wiglaf wondered, *when I have so cruelly killed a ...uh...?*

"I'll take that!" growled the coach.

Wiglaf looked up to see a very bald Coach Plungett snatch the hairy thing from the end of Surekill and angrily set it on his head.

Only then did Wiglaf understand what creature he had murdered. Coach Plungett's own brown pageboy wig!

# Chapter 6

Wiglaf picked at his lunch of boiled eel on a bun. Coach Plungett was sure to give him an F in slaying now. He had messed up royally— and on his very first day of school.

"Come on, Wiglaf. Eat up!" Angus told him. "You do *not* want to be late for Mordred's class."

*Mordred!* Wiglaf shuddered. *What would the headmaster do to a new boy who had nearly slayed the slaying coach?*

With dark thoughts, Wiglaf followed Angus to a stone-walled classroom. As the boys sat down on a rickety bench, a huge man in a red cloak strode through the door. Thick black hair sprouted from his head. His violet eyes bulged like overripe plums.

"Atten-*tion!*" Mordred the Marvelous called.

The students leaped to their feet. Wiglaf did, too.

"At ease!" Mordred commanded.

The boys sat down.

"Let us review," the headmaster said. "Why are you here at Dragon Slayers' Academy?"

"To learn to slay evil dragons!" Eric called out at once. "To make the world safe for little children! To save villagers from—"

"Yes, yes," Mordred interrupted, holding up a hand heavy with gold rings. "That is all well and good. But what about yesterday's lesson? What did I say? Anyone? Baldrick?"

A small freckle-faced boy with a runny nose stood up. "We are here to learn how to get a dragon's golden hoard, sir! And bring it back to you, sir!"

"Correct!" Mordred grinned, showing a shiny gold front tooth. "To bring me gold! And"—he coughed—"to take some...a teeny bit...maybe...home to your"—he coughed again—"parents."

He cleared his throat. "Now, who remembers how to find a cave-dwelling dragon?"

Again, Eric was the first to answer. "Look for burned spots on shrubs and bushes!" he called. "And big footprints with three long toes!"

Mordred nodded. "And when you spot the dragon...what must you look out for?"

"Beware flames of death!" Eric shouted. "Beware a dragon's poison spit!"

"Correct, Eric." Mordred sighed and looked around. "Anyone *else?*"

"Beware the eyes that never close!" Eric called again. "Beware the knife-sharp teeth! Beware the powerful, lashing tail!"

"Thank you, *Eric*," Mordred said. "Now,

what else must a dragon hunter know in order to *slay* such a beast?"

"How to talk to a dragon!" Eric called. "How to be brave!"

Mordred nodded. "Anything else?"

At last Eric was quiet. And so were all the other boys.

But Wiglaf had listened well to the minstrel's dragon tales. He knew there was one thing that Eric had not mentioned. Timidly, he raised his hand.

Mordred's bulging eyes lit on him. "Ah, the new boy! The one who scalped Coach Plungett!" The headmaster chuckled. "So, new boy, what else should a dragon hunter know?"

"A dragon's secret weakness?" Wiglaf said meekly.

"That's right!" Mordred's eyebrows shot up.

"Oh, everybody knows *that*," Eric complained.

"Let the new boy tell what he knows of dragon secrets, Eric," Mordred said. "Maybe you will learn something."

"From *him?*" Eric muttered. "Not likely."

"Well, new boy?" Mordred said. "Pray, tell us what you know!"

"I—I know very little...." Wiglaf began.

"See?" Eric cut in. "What did I tell you?"

But the headmaster ignored him. "New boy," he said, "know you the secret weakness of the dragon Gorzil?"

"No, sir," Wiglaf answered. "His weakness is still a secret."

"Too true." Mordred sighed sadly. "But it would be useful to know it. For Gorzil is rumored to be in the Dark Forest. My scout Yorick is there now. As soon as he finds Gorzil's cave, I shall send my best boys out to slay him. Slay him, and claim his great big golden hoard!"

These words were barely out of Mordred's

mouth when a small man burst into the class-room. Branches and leaves were tied to his tunic, as if he were trying to disguise himself as a bush.

"Yorick!" Mordred exclaimed. "Back so soon? What news from the Dark Forest?"

"My lord," Yorick began, "Gorzil has moved to a cave outside the village of Toe-nail."

"Toenail!" Torblad shrieked. "My family lives in Toenail!"

"Sit down, Torblad," Mordred snarled. "Go on, Yorick."

"My lord," Yorick said, "the Toenailians have brought Gorzil all their gold. Now he swears to burn Toenail to the ground unless a son and a daughter of the village are outside his cave tomorrow. Tomorrow at dawn, in time for breakfast!"

"Oh, that's nice of Gorzil," Torblad said, cheering up. "Having company for breakfast."

"You ninny!" Mordred cried. "They are to *be* his breakfast!" The headmaster turned back to his scout. "So! I shall send boys out to slay Gorzil this very afternoon!"

Then a look of horror crossed his face.

"Egad!" he exclaimed. "Class II and Class III just left on that blasted field trip to see the petrified dragon skeleton! That means I shall have to send Class I boys!"

"Pray, send me!" Eric cried, falling to his knees.

"Yes, yes," Mordred said. "But remember, we have a buddy system here. I'll need another volunteer." He looked around the room. "Anyone but Angus. If I sent you, I'd never hear the end of it from your mother. All right, who will it be?"

No hands went up.

"Come now," Mordred coaxed. "Gorzil is not so bad!"

Still no hands went up.

"My patience grows thin!" Mordred warned. Then his violet eyes lit upon Wiglaf.

"You! New boy!" he boomed. "You seem to know a fair bit about dragons. And I chanced to look at the register book at lunchtime. You never paid your seven pennies!"

"That is so," Wiglaf began. "But—" He stopped. He had promised Frypot to say not a word about their dishwashing deal.

"No buts!" Mordred cried. "You shall go with Eric! And you shall pay your seven pennies out of Gorzil's gold!"

"Aw, sir!" Eric cried. "Pray, pick someone else! Wiglaf has not even been here a whole day! He knows nothing of slaying!"

"*You* slay Gorzil, then!" Mordred shouted. "Let him pull the cart for the dragon's hoard. Now, be off! You must reach Gorzil's cave by dawn. What are you waiting for? Go!"

# Chapter 7

eady, Wiglaf?" Eric called as he hurried toward the gatehouse.

Wiglaf was bent over, trying to fix a wobbly wheel on the hoard cart. He glanced up and was nearly blinded by the glare from Eric's slaying outfit.

Eric stood proudly before him in a gleaming silver helmet. He carried a broad silver shield. And a wide silver belt held his sword.

Wiglaf had only Surekill.

"What fine gear," Wiglaf told Eric.

"Yes," Eric agreed. "I sent away for it from the Sir Lancelot Fan Club catalog. Come! You shall pull the cart as Mordred said. Let us be off. My sword is itching to slay the dragon!"

Wiglaf began to slide back the great iron bolt on the gatehouse door. But a yell from Eric made him stop.

"Boar!" Eric cried. "Wild boar!"

Wiglaf turned to see Eric with his sword drawn and his shield up.

"Stand back!" Eric shouted. "I shall slay the charging beast!"

"What beast?" Wiglaf asked. Then he spotted something running toward them across the castle yard. It was Daisy!

"Eric, stop!" Wiglaf shouted. "Stop! That is my own pig, Daisy!"

Eric stopped and glumly lowered his sword. He jammed it back into its scabbard and stomped off, grumbling.

Wiglaf ran to Daisy.

"Iglaf-Way!" she squealed. "Ake-tay ee-may ith-way ou-yay!"

"I cannot, Daisy," Wiglaf said sadly. He squatted down beside her and scratched her bristly ears. "It is too dangerous. For I am off to hunt a dragon."

"Orzil-Gay?" Daisy's voice trembled.

Wiglaf nodded. "Who knows? Perhaps I shall return a hero." He tried to smile. "But if I do not"—he gulped—"if I do not return, I am sure Frypot will take good care of you. Now I—I must go. Farewell, best pig in the world!"

"Arewell-fay, Iglaf-Way!" Daisy called after him. "Ood-gay uck-lay!"

Wiglaf waved and hurried back to the gatehouse. Then he picked up the cart handle. "Let us be off," he said to Eric.

Wiglaf and Eric followed the trail down the hill from Dragon Slayers' Academy. Then they headed north on Huntsman's Path.

They walked beside the Swampy River all afternoon. Strange birds cried out from the stunted trees along the way. Hairy-legged spiders dropped down on them from over-hanging branches. Once an angry troll threatened them with his club. But Wiglaf was not afraid. The thought of facing Gorzil was so terrifying that nothing else bothered him.

Well, almost nothing.

"I shall slay Gorzil, no problem!" Eric announced for the two-hundredth time. "I shall plunge my sword into his throat. I shall twist it! Buckets of blood will gush from the dragon's steaming wound! Then I shall—"

"You know," Wiglaf broke in finally, "my sword was made for dragon slaying, too."

"That bent-up old thing?" Eric sneered.

Wiglaf nodded. "A wizard gave it to me," he explained. "When I say magic words, it will leap from my hand and obey."

Eric looked doubtful. "And just what are the magic words?"

"Uh...the wizard had forgotten," Wiglaf mumbled.

"It matters not," Eric scoffed as they came to a fork in Huntsman's Path. One path led to the village of Toenail. The other led into the Dark Forest. "For I shall slay this dragon with my own silvery sword. I shall cut Gorzil to ribbons! I shall—"

Suddenly, Eric stopped talking. He stared at the blackened leaves of a nearby shrub.

"Behold!" he cried. "This bush is scorched!"

Wiglaf bent down to take a closer look. "So it is," he agreed. "Could it be from the hot breath of a dragon?"

"How could it not? And look here!" Eric pointed to the ground. "Footprints!"

Wiglaf stared at a huge three-toed print in the path in front of them. "My, but these foot-prints are large!" he exclaimed.

"Come!" Eric said. "They will lead us to

Gorzil's cave. Hark!" he added. "What noise is that?"

Wiglaf listened. "It sounds like someone crying."

The sound grew louder. Then a boy and girl about Wiglaf and Eric's age came along on the path from Toenail. Tears streamed down their cheeks.

"What ails you, good travelers?" Eric called to them. "And how can we help?"

"Alackaday!" the boy wailed. "You cannot help us. No one can! My sister Zelda and I are on our way to Gorzil's cave!"

"Do you mean," Wiglaf began, "that you are the son and daughter of the village? That you are to be Gorzil's...breakfast?"

Zelda nodded. "I fear it is so. The Toenail village masters held a lottery. And alas— Gawain and I won!"

"If only a brave knight would slay Gorzil

and save us!" Gawain said. "But there is no hope of that."

Eric yanked his sword from its scabbard and held it high in the air.

"Fear not, young friends," he cried. "Eric the Dragon Slayer is at your service!"

Gawain and Zelda stared at him.

"You?" Zelda said.

Eric nodded.

"You are but a boy!" she scoffed.

Eric sniffed. "I am first in my class at Dragon Slayers' Academy," he replied. "I shall slay Gorzil—no sweat!"

"Do you know how many brave knights have tried and perished in his flames?" Gawain asked.

"Um...no. But—" Eric began.

"Gorzil will toast you like a marshmallow!" Zelda declared. "Unless," she added, "you come up with a clever plan."

"A plan?" Wiglaf said. "What kind of—"

"Change clothes with us," Zelda cut in. "Disguise yourselves as the son and the daughter of Toenail and catch Gorzil off guard!"

At first, Eric looked doubtful. Then he begain to smile. "Yes!" he exclaimed. "I can see it now! At dawn, *we* shall appear at the mouth of Gorzil's cave, dressed in your clothing. Gorzil will never suspect that behind my back I have a sword! When the dragon opens his jaws to eat me, I shall whip out my sword and plunge it deep into his throat. His whole body will shudder and—"

"But Eric," Wiglaf broke in. "How can one of *us* pass for a *daughter* of the village?"

But Eric was already taking off his helmet. "Worry not, Wiglaf," he said. "Just be quick and give your tunic to Gawain. Here, Zelda. Take my Sir Lancelot armor." Eric handed the girl his helmet and chain mail. "As soon as we are dressed in their clothes," Eric told Wiglaf, "we shall go thitherward to carry out our plan!"

# Chapter 8

he sun dawned on Wiglaf and Eric outside the mouth of Gorzil's cave. With trembling fingers, Wiglaf finished tying his lucky rag to Surekill's hilt. If ever he needed luck, it was now!

Wiglaf adjusted Gawain's baggy tunic and trousers. Then he glanced over at Eric, who was wearing Zelda's sky-blue dress. His brown hair peeked out from under her white lace cap.

"I was wrong to think you would not pass for a daughter of the village, Eric," Wiglaf said.

Eric only nodded.

"That lace cap suits you," Wiglaf went on. "If I were a dragon, I should believe you were a girl—and a fetching one, at that."

"Enough!" Eric snapped. "Keep your thoughts on Gorzil!"

Just then a cloud of smoke billowed out of the cave, and a voice inside boomed, "I SMELL BREAKFAST!"

Wiglaf and Eric hid their swords behind their backs as a huge, green, snakelike head poked out from the smoke. The dragon's eyes blazed orange. Steam rose from his jaws. Yellow slime dripped from his nose. Wiglaf had never seen anything so hideous.

So this was Gorzil! Wiglaf thought back to the minstrel's tale. He gripped his sword more tightly. He hoped that Gorzil would not soon be using Surekill for his toothpick!

Gorzil puffed two smoke rings from his nose. "What luck!" he exclaimed. "Here are a

tasty little son and daughter of the village. And here is Gorzil, hungry for breakfast! Daughter, have you any last words to say to Gorzil?"

Eric took a step forward. He whispered something. But even Wiglaf could not hear what it was.

"What? What?" Gorzil said. "Speak up, girl!" But Eric only whispered again.

The dragon stepped out from the cave. Slime trickled from his nose. It spattered on the ground in greasy yellow puddles. He lowered his head close to Eric. "Now Gorzil can hear better. What did you say, my delicious cookie?"

"I AM NOT YOUR COOKIE, GORZIL!" Eric shouted into the dragon's ear. "I AM YOUR WORST NIGHTMARE!" And he whipped his sword from behind his back.

An angry red crest rose from Gorzil's head.

Sparks shot from his nose. They scorched the hem of Eric's dress. Then Gorzil raised the tip of his tail over his head and whacked Eric's sword out of his hand.

Wiglaf and Eric watched it sail off into the woods.

"Uh-oh," said Eric. He ducked behind a nearby boulder. "Quick, Wiglaf!" he called. "Draw your sword!"

Wiglaf stared up at the monster before him. He tried to remember what he had learned in his one-and-only slaying class. But Gorzil was no dummy dragon with a target painted under his chin. He was the real thing!

With a quivering hand, Wiglaf brought Surekill out from behind his back.

The dragon gazed at the rusty thing and chuckled.

"Surekill," Wiglaf said, "slay the dragon!"

Surekill did not move.

"Surekill!" Wiglaf tried again. "Do the dragon in!"

Surekill made no thrust.

Yellow flames began to flicker from Gorzil's nostrils.

"Surekill!" Wiglaf yelled. "HELP!"

In the blink of an eye, the sword leaped out of Wiglaf's hand. It glowed red hot as it soared up, up into the air. Gorzil stopped flaming. Wiglaf and Eric and the dragon all stared as Surekill rose higher and higher into the clouds. They waited for it to reappear. But the sword had vanished.

At last, Gorzil fixed his gaze back on Wiglaf. "Too bad," he chortled. "Now it is breakfast time!"

Gorzil opened his terrible jaws. Any second, Wiglaf knew, lightning bolts would strike him!

*If only I had more time!* he thought. *Time*

enough to discover Gorzil's secret weakness! But how? Wiglaf racked his brain. But he could think of nothing. Nothing!

At last, Wiglaf opened his mouth, and over Gorzil's thundering roar, he yelled the first thing that came to his mind: "Knock! Knock!"

Instantly, the thunder stopped.

"A joke!" the dragon cried. "There's nothing Gorzil likes better than a good joke! Breakfast can wait. All right....Who's there?"

"Lettuce," Wiglaf managed.

"Lettuce?" Gorzil snorted a puff of smoke. "Lettuce? Gorzil can guess! Easy! Oh, foo. Lettuce who?"

"Lettuce alone!" Wiglaf answered.

"Oooooh," Gorzil groaned. "That was a bad joke."

"Really bad," Eric called from behind the rock.

"Gorzil *hates* bad jokes," the dragon added.

In fact, Wiglaf thought that the dragon looked slightly ill.

"Try again, son of the village," Gorzil ordered. "Tell Gorzil another joke. But make it a good one!"

"All right," Wiglaf said. "Knock! Knock!"

The dragon perked up. "Gorzil will get this one! Who's there?"

"Arthur!" cried Wiglaf.

"Arthur? Hmm. Oh, yes! Oh, poo. Arthur who?"

Wiglaf answered, "Arthur any dragons uglier than you?"

"Aghh!" Gorzil cried. "That was even worse!"

Wiglaf noticed that Gorzil's bright orange eyes had faded. His scales were no longer a brilliant green. The dragon looked the way Wiglaf felt when he heard too many of Fergus's knock-knocks: Sick.

Suddenly Wiglaf had a hunch. Could it be?

His heart began to race with excitement.

"Knock! Knock!" Wiglaf said again.

"Who's there?" Gorzil mumbled.

"Howard!" called Wiglaf.

"How—Howard who?" Gorzil asked weakly.

Wiglaf yelled, "Howard you like to hear another rotten joke?"

"Another? Uggghh!" The dragon gasped for air. He clutched at his scaly chest with his claws.

Quickly, Wiglaf struck again: "Knock! Knock!"

"Who...there?" Gorzil's head was drooping now.

"Ivan!" Wiglaf shouted.

"Iv...whooo...?" Gorzil's legs buckled under him. He hit the ground.

"Ivan to stay alive!" Wiglaf cried.

That did it. Gorzil's chest heaved. His tail lashed one final time and was still. His tongue flopped out the side of his mouth and lay in a puddle of yellow drool. Then, with a thunderous poof, Gorzil's body exploded into a cloud of dragon dust.

Eric hiked up his skirt and ran through the dust to Wiglaf's side.

"By Lancelot's lance!" he exclaimed. "Gorzil is dead!"

Then all at once, Wiglaf heard a wild roar. He turned to see hundreds of cheering villagers popping out from behind rocks and trees. Villagers who had come to watch them fight the dragon!

Joyfully, the villagers began rushing toward them. Wiglaf brushed the dragon dust from his tunic. He readied himself to be lifted up onto their shoulders. To be carried through Toenail, a hero!

"Out of me way!" a villager shouted gruffly, shoving past him. A stampede of villagers followed on his heels.

Wiglaf and Eric had to leap behind a

boulder or be trampled as the whole crowd charged straight into the cave—straight for Gorzil's hoard.

As the two dragon hunters stood staring, a flash lit the sky. Wiglaf looked up just in time to see Surekill tumble from the clouds—down into a clump of weeds.

"Nice try, Surekill," said Wiglaf.

# Chapter 9

"Did the villagers have to grab every last bit of Gorzil's hoard?" Eric grumbled.

By this time, Eric had fetched his sword, and Wiglaf and Eric had found Gawain and Zelda and switched clothes again. Eric told Zelda he was sorry about the burned spots on her dress. But she was so loaded with gold, she did not seem to mind at all.

Now Wiglaf and Eric were back on the path to DSA. This time Eric pulled the cart.

"I am all for taking from the rich and giving to the poor," Eric went on. "But could not the villagers have left us a few gold coins?

How shall we ever face Mordred empty-handed?"

"Gorzil stole from the villagers," Wiglaf reminded him. "It seems only fair that they should get their gold back."

"I suppose," muttered Eric. And with a sigh he dragged the cart over a rocky patch of ground.

"Are you sure you want to pull the cart?" Wiglaf asked him.

"It is the least I can do," Eric told Wiglaf. "For in truth, you did slay the mighty dragon."

Wiglaf blushed on hearing Eric's words. "I could never have done it without you, Eric," he said. "It was a clever plan—and you surely fooled Gorzil into thinking you were a girl."

For a moment, Eric was silent. Then he stopped and turned to Wiglaf. "There is something I should like to tell you," he said gravely.

"Pray, tell," Wiglaf answered.

"'Tis a secret," Eric warned him. "Will you swear to keep it?"

"I swear it on my sword," Wiglaf promised. He lifted Surekill into the air.

"My real name," Eric told him, "is Erica."

"Egad!" Wiglaf exclaimed. "Your parents gave you a girl's name?"

"No! I *am* a girl, you ninny. In fact, I am a princess. Princess Erica, daughter of Queen Barb and King Ken."

Wiglaf's mouth dropped open.

"I always longed for a life of adventure," Erica explained. "When I saw the notice for Dragon Slayers' Academy, I begged my parents to let me go. At last they agreed. But when I arrived at school, Frypot said Mordred would never admit a girl. It was good old Frypot's plan to dress me as a boy.

He keeps my secret. And in return, I empty his eel traps."

"Zounds!" Wiglaf exclaimed. Then he added, "Forgive me, your highness."

"None of that highness stuff!" the princess growled. She drew her silvery sword and waved it at Wiglaf. "You must call me only Eric! And do not slip up! No one at school must know my secret. Not until I get my Dragon Slayers' Academy diploma. If you tell anyone, I shall make you very, very sorry!"

"I shall never say a word," Wiglaf promised. "And if I do, you may tell *my* secret."

"Your secret?" asked Erica.

"See this lucky rag tied to the hilt of my sword?" Wiglaf asked. "It is...uh...the last bit of my baby blanket."

Erica smiled. "Indeed! That is not something that you would want to get around." She gave a yank to the cart handle and started down the path again.

"Now," Erica went on, "let us go over the story we shall tell back at DSA. Since we have no gold, we must make the most of our adventure."

"A fine idea," Wiglaf agreed.

"I think," Erica began, "that we shall start by telling how I bravely lured Gorzil out of his cave. And how I scared him near to death when I brandished my silvery sword! Then, when he least expected it..."

As Eric—make that Erica—talked on, Wiglaf let his own thoughts wander. He had become a hero—just as the minstrel had said he would. And without spilling a single drop of blood!

*Daisy would be so proud of me*, Wiglaf thought. And wouldn't Fergus and Molwena and his twelve unwashed brothers be surprised when they learned that he was indeed Wiglaf of Pinwick, Dragon Slayer!

# Find out what new adventures await our hero in:

## Dragon Slayers' Academy ™ 2

### REVENGE OF THE DRAGON LADY

*"Spineless, gutless, weak-kneed brat!*
*Chicken-hearted scaredy-cat!*
*Cringing coward, yellow-belly,*
*Lily-livered, heart of jelly!*
*Change this Wiglaf, standing here,*
*Into He-Who-Knows-No-Fear!"*

Is a wizard's spell for courage enough to save Wiglaf when the "Mother of all Dragons" (or at least the mother of 3,684 of them) comes looking for the lad who slayed son #92? Wiglaf better hope so—because she's big...she's bad ...and she's very, very mad!